Silent Samurai and the
Magnificent Rescue

By Eileen Wacker • Illustrated by Alan M. Low

ISBN 978-1-4392743-5-5

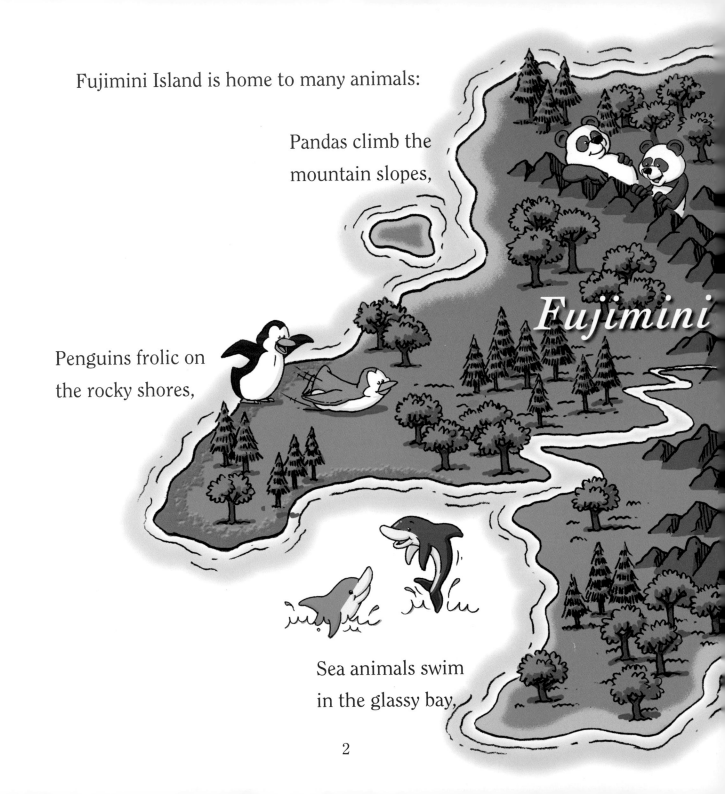

Fujimini Island is home to many animals:

Pandas climb the
mountain slopes,

Penguins frolic on
the rocky shores,

Fujimini

Sea animals swim
in the glassy bay,

2

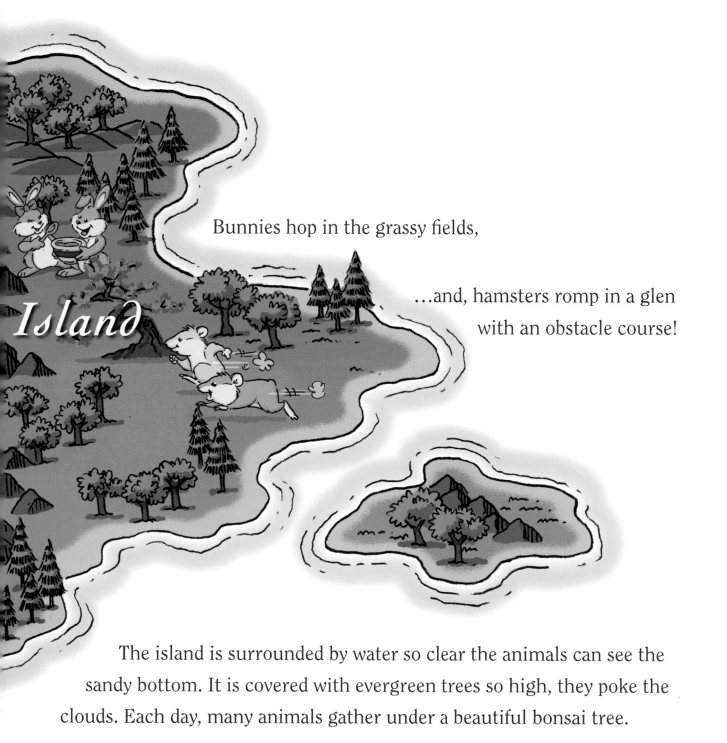

Bunnies hop in the grassy fields,

...and, hamsters romp in a glen
with an obstacle course!

Island

The island is surrounded by water so clear the animals can see the sandy bottom. It is covered with evergreen trees so high, they poke the clouds. Each day, many animals gather under a beautiful bonsai tree.

Today, Purple Penguin hurries over to the bonsai tree, waiting for the others to arrive. He is flapping his flippers and making a commotion. He keeps squawking, "I have big news. I have really big news!"

Brown Hamster, Black Panda and Blue Bunny go to the bonsai tree to hear the news. Purple Penguin says, "Finally, you are here! I just heard from Blue Bay Dolphin that Samurai and a raft carrying their equipment are approaching Fujimini Island! They must be on a special mission. Isn't this exciting? It's like royalty coming to visit! Please go back and tell everyone we must plan an amazing welcome party."

Purple Penguin is so excited he doesn't notice that the others are not happy. They are quietly concerned that the Samurai may have come for a battle.

Brown Hamster goes back to the glen and reports to the other hamsters. "Purple Penguin says that Samurai warriors are coming for some special, secret mission."

Green Hamster immediately thinks about holding one of their shiny swords.

Pink Hamster suggests a party with cake.

Brown Hamster quietly wonders if they should prepare for a party or a sword fight.

"I think we should stay here and let the others greet the Samurai until we know what their mission is," says Brown Hamster. "There could be trouble. They are warriors after all."

"If there is trouble, we can always run away," offers Blue Hamster. "Since we run Hamster Races every day, we are very fast." Brown Hamster responds, "Yes, but we just run in circles so it might be easy to catch us!"

Green Hamster whispers, "I just have to hold one of those shiny swords. We're going!"

Over in the grassy field, the bunnies are also worried about the arrival of the warriors. "Why are they coming?" they ask. "Let everyone else meet them first." Orange Bunny, the island's *taekwondo* instructor says, "We are taught to fight only when there is no other option. But just in case, we should practice our *taekwondo* exercises all morning." Later, they plan to hop to hiding places and watch the visitors' arrival.

The pandas also discuss the news of the visitors. Brown Panda says, "I heard Samurai are good hiders. They may try to take our best trees to set up an attack." Black Panda agrees, "I am not sure I want them to come. Let's stay up on the mountain and watch."

Yellow Panda runs into the woods throwing firecrackers, shouting, "I'm going to scare away the bad luck. Bang Bang! Go away bad luck!" Orange Panda starts making giant bowls of noodles saying, "With warriors coming, we'll need long noodles for a long life!"

9

Purple Penguin is confused as he watches the animals prepare for the Samurai arrival and says to Red Penguin, "What a commotion. We should be preparing gifts and a special welcome party. This is not honorable. The Samurai will think we are impolite."

Red Penguin nods her agreement but all of a sudden she hears Blue Bay Dolphin in the distance making loud clacking noises. "Something must be wrong. Let's ask Blue Whale to go out and investigate."

They call out to the reclusive Blue Whale who swims over excitedly. He is so happy to be included that he is flapping his big flippers up and down. "Blue Whale, please calm down! You are splashing everyone."

"Sorry, I can do this. I want to help!" exclaims the Blue Whale. "Give me a chance. I won't even stop for a snack." He sets off to find out why the Blue Bay Dolphin is making clacking noises.

Shortly after, Blue Whale returns and reports, "The boat carrying the Tortoise Samurai's equipment is sinking after being hit by a storm. They are swimming next to the boat, trying to hold it up. But they can't keep it floating much longer."

Purple Penguin starts panicking. He is hopping, flapping and squawking, "Aaaacckk! Aaaacckk! The Samurai are in trouble!"

Other animals come over to see what all the fuss is about and hear the news about the sinking equipment.

The animals start talking all at once. "Surely the tortoises know how to swim?" exclaims Orange Bunny. "Is their equipment too heavy? Will their swords sink like stones?" Green Hamster asks. Purple Penguin just says, "Oh dear! I don't know. Tortoises can swim, but they must need their equipment for the special mission."

Black Panda takes charge and says, "Okay everyone, we need to do something." Suddenly the animals run, scamper and hop toward the penguin coast. They decide to work together to strengthen a raft to rescue the Samurai's equipment. Then the tortoises can safely swim to shore on their own.

The pandas are very strong and gather giant branches. "Hamsters," they cry, "Use your paws to twist vines into rope and bind the branches!" The hamsters run and bind in unison. The raft is getting stronger.

The bunnies use their *taekwondo* moves to break branches quickly as Orange Bunny shouts, *"Hana, tul, set!"* Everyone is impressed and Green Hamster secretly vows to practice his *taekwondo* kicks more.

They quickly finish the raft. The penguins, who are at the water's edge, call out to Blue Whale, "Pull the raft to the Samurai! Then tow the equipment to shore."

The Samurai silently stare at the animals as they approach. The animals jump to the broken boat and start moving the equipment.

Blue Bay Dolphin is clicking, "Hurry! Save the equipment before it sinks!"

The quiet Tortoise Samurai don't say anything. They just swim along silently next to the raft and the animals.

When they reach the shore, the animals gather to get a closer look at Black Tortoise Samurai. His face is a little fierce but also friendly and kind. His eyes twinkle with mischief, making him appear fun.

"Wow, they are not scary after all, but they sure don't talk a lot," whispers Green Hamster, "And, look at those swords!"

Black Tortoise Samurai clears his throat. "We were sent on a special mission to solve the mystery of the Dynasty Dragon. We would have lost our equipment without your magnificent rescue."

Green Hamster asks, "Quiet Mr. Warrior, is part of your mission to attack us? Have you come for a sword fight?" The other animals hold their breath, surprised that Green Hamster asked, but wondering the same thing.

"Oh, my goodness," replies Black Tortoise Samurai, "we are not here to fight anyone! We are only here to search for something very special for the Emperor."

All the animals start dancing and cheering. Blue Bunny shouts, "Let's have a party under the bonsai tree to welcome our new friends." Everyone agrees that would be fun.

The pandas rush to get the long noodles and firecrackers for the celebration. The bunnies offer to have a *taekwondo* show for the Samurai and bring a cake. Purple Penguin is very proud and makes an announcement. "Honorable Samurai, we are humbled by your visit. Please accept our simple feast and performance as a sign of our friendship."

Black Tortoise Samurai lets Green Hamster touch the shiny sword. "Maybe you will grow up to be a warrior someday," he says. "Today you were all warriors. Thank you for your kindness and open welcome. Tomorrow we shall discuss how to repay your kindness." The Samurai bow to the animals.

22

Brown Hamster says, "It was wise to welcome new friends even if they are Samurai warriors. We worked well as a team and great things happened. It is one of the best days on Fujimini Island! Let's rest up. Who knows, the Samurai may need our help solving the mystery of the Dynasty Dragon."

Everyone laughs and waves goodnight to their new friends, ready to sleep. And, Green and Pink Hamster bow to the friendly Black Tortoise Samurai and skip back to the glen. Along the way, they make a secret pact to join the special mission.